Mia and the
Rocket Ship Tree

Written and Illustrated by
Boaz Gavish

Koalabo Publishing

Fonts used include Arial and Harimau by Hanoded of https://www.hanodedfonts.com/
A Desktop license for Harimau was purchased via https://www.fontspring.com
which grants the creation of commercial graphics and documents.

978-1-9997532-1-4   Koalabo Publishing

This Book Belongs To:

_____

Made with love for Mia.

Love yourself first and others will too;
You are always enough, no matter what you do.

Mia put on her spacesuit and
took her robot Koalabo by the hand,
which made Koalabo wonder,
What kind of adventure
will Mia want to have today?

In the park past her
garden, Mia's friends
were playing all kinds
of games, running around,
making a terrific noise.

"Ready to join us for
Space Games?"
Mia asked her friends.

"Not again!" they shouted.
"Come play with us instead."

"But I can't run around
in my space suit,"
Mia answered.
"I want to have an adventure!"

"Let's go to our special tree instead," Suggested Koalabo in his cold robotic voice.

Like every koala robot, he knew the secret to having the best adventures.

"That could be a lot of fun," Mia said and scrambled up the ladder to her tree house...

Koalabo bounced up
the tree behind her.

Mia put her wooden key
into the tree trunk and
turned it three times.

The tree started changing slowly...

...into a rocket ship tree!

Mia saw flashes of fire shoot out of the branches and lots of knobs and buttons popped out of the trunk.

She knew just what Koalabo

was going to say next.

"Three, two, one... lift-off!" shouted Koalabo.

Mia flicked the switches to fire the main engine.

She was excited that her adventure was about to begin!

The tree slowly lifted off
the ground with a big

and then burst through the
clouds with a wonderful

Mia felt like she was on top of the world!

Quick as a
sneeze,

Mia and
Koalabo were
in space.

They were
flying faster than
the fastest airplane,
leaving Earth far,
far behind...

Through the window, the moon appeared bigger and bigger, brighter and brighter.

"Is the moon made of cheese?" asked Mia.

"Wouldn't that be wonderful?" answered Koalabo.

On they flew,
past the fishy Fish-teroids.

The Fish-teroids
didn't stop to say hello.
They were off on one of
their own adventures!

They flew past magnificent planets,

some with rings

and some without.

Past a flying swimming pool
full of happy green creatures
splashing about.

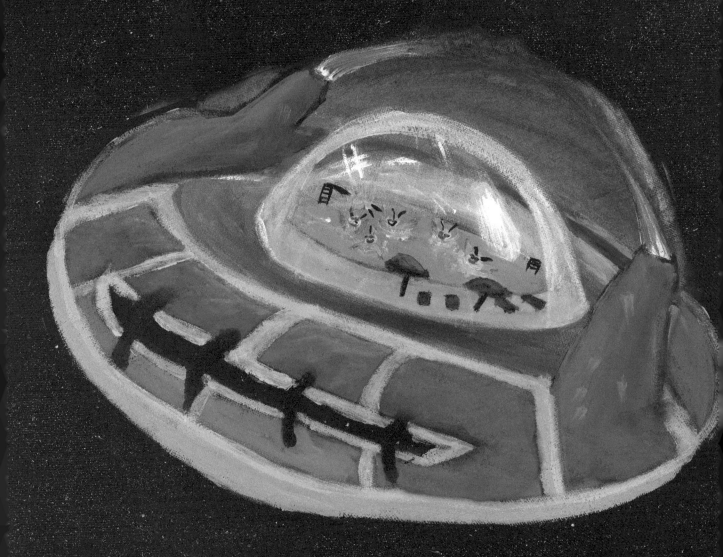

Past stars and
other Space Delights.

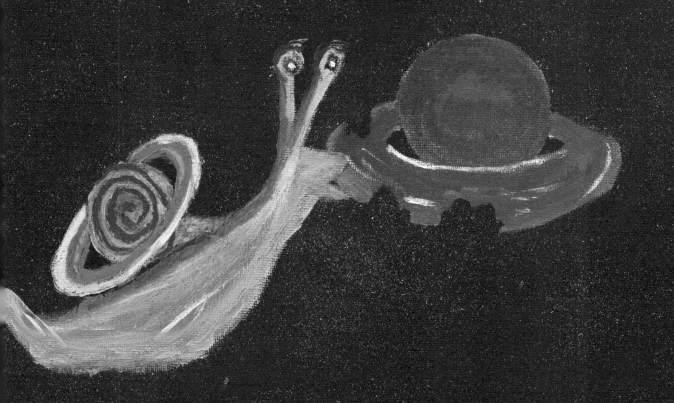

Past a fiery green sun,

so dazzling and bright.

Until they reached the home of
the Space Ticklers
on a small purple planet.

"You can't play with us,"
yelled one of the Space Ticklers,

as they all
ran around tickling
each other.

But Mia could not wait to prove to them how good she was at tickling!

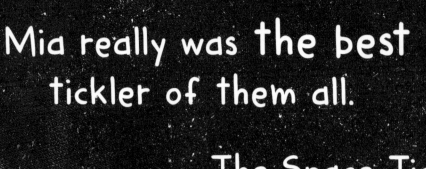

Mia really was **the best** tickler of them all.

The Space Ticklers were delighted when they saw Mia was their new **tickle champion.**

...and
tickled...

Tickle

Tickle

Tickle

After a while,
Mia got bored with
all the tickling.

It seemed
to be all the
Space Ticklers
wanted to do.

"Tickling is
the best game!"
they cried out,

but Mia wondered what
her friends were doing instead.

Suddenly, a soft sound
came from the tree:

"Mia! Mia!
Where are you?
We want to play!"

It sounded like Mia's friends
calling to her from far, far away.

Now is a good time
to fly back home, Mia decided.

"Goodbye Space Ticklers,"
Mia shouted.

But the Space Ticklers did not want to
let their best tickler leave their planet.

So they sent
super sticky rainbow tickles
at her until she was stuck
and unable to move.

But the rainbow tickles
did not work on Koalabo.

His robot body couldn't
feel the tickles at all!

Koalabo showered a burst of tickles
on the Space Ticklers, so that
they couldn't move.

"Chop-chop!"
Koalabo freed Mia from
the rainbow tickles and
they raced back up
into the tree house.

"Lift off,"
shouted Mia and
off they flew...

...through the
darkness of space
and past planets and stars.
Past the moon and the sun,
who were having such fun...

...softly they fell...
through candy peach clouds

and
pink vanilla
skies...

...until they reached Mia's garden. And Mia's friends were still there, asking her to play with them.

Mia thought about her fun adventures in space and the naughty Space Ticklers. She was very happy to be back with her true friends.

So she took off
her spacesuit and
joined them!

CPSIA information can be obtained
at www.ICGtesting.com
Printed in the USA
BVHW02n1510030518
515213BV00018B/247/P

* 9 7 8 1 9 9 9 7 5 3 2 1 4 *